Syd Hoff's Henrietta Stories

Dover Children's Classics

Syd Hoff's Henrietta Stories

Including *Henrietta Lays Some Eggs, Henrietta, the Early Bird,*
and *Henrietta Goes to the Fair*

Syd Hoff

Dover Publications, Inc.
Mineola, New York

Dover Publications would like to thank
Carol Edmonston for her assistance.

Bibliographical Note

Syd Hoff's Henrietta Stories, first published by Dover Publications, Inc., in 2016,
is a republication of the following works by Syd Hoff and all originally published
by Garrard Publishing Company, Champaign, Illinois: *Henrietta Lays Some Eggs*
(1977); *Henrietta, the Early Bird* (1978); and *Henrietta Goes to the Fair* (1979).

International Standard Book Number
ISBN-13: 978-0-486-80025-7
ISBN-10: 0-486-80025-3

Manufactured in the United States by RR Donnelley
80025301   2016
www.doverpublications.com

Contents

Henrietta
Lays Some Eggs

Henrietta Lays Some Eggs

It was morning
on the farm.
"Come on, everybody,"
Mr. Gray called
to his chickens.
"Get into the truck," he said.
"We are going to market."

3

One chicken
did not want to go.
Her name was Henrietta.

"I think I'll stay here,"
Henrietta said.
"I like it on the farm."

"No," said Mr. Gray.
"You get into the truck.
It is a long way
to the city."

"I love to ride,"
Henrietta said.
"But I don't want
to be the chicken
on a plate
with mashed potatoes."

Henrietta flew
out of the truck.

But a chicken
cannot fly very far.
She came down
in the pigpen.

"May I stay here?"
Henrietta asked.
"Yes," said the pigs.
"But soon we will
be going to market, too."

Henrietta left
in a hurry.

"Cluck, cluck," she said
as she walked along.

Henrietta came
to the duck pond.

"You can't stay here
unless you say quack, quack,"
said the ducks.

"I can't swim anyway,"
said Henrietta.
She walked on.

She came to a place
where some men
were making a fire.

"You're just in time
for dinner," said the men.
"What are we having?"
asked Henrietta.

"WE'RE having chicken,"
the men said.
"Not ME!" said Henrietta.

Quickly she flew
into the woods.

Soon she met
a hungry fox.

Henrietta had never seen
a fox before.
"Are you a dog?"
she asked.
"Yes," said the fox.

"Then bark for me,"
said Henrietta.
The fox tried to bark.
"You don't bark
like a dog," she said.

"Maybe you are a cat,"
said Henrietta.
"Yes, that's what I am,"
said the hungry fox.
He tried to meow.
"Meow, meeow, meoow."

"You don't sound
like a cat,"
said Henrietta.

"Then I guess
I'm a hungry fox!"
said the fox.
He tried to catch Henrietta.

But she got away.
"I'd better get out
of the woods,"
thought Henrietta.

She walked
all the way to the city.

Cars were tooting.
"Beep, beep," they went.
"I used to say
'peep, peep'
when I first came
out of my shell,"
thought Henrietta.

"Please go
when the sign says WALK,"
said a policeman.
"When will it say FLY?"
asked Henrietta.

She went into a park.
A man was feeding
some birds.
"May I eat, too?"
asked Henrietta.

But the food
was all gone.

"Come fly with us
to the top of the building,"
said the birds.
"I can't fly that high,"
said Henrietta.
"I would have
to take the elevator."

Henrietta went on
down the street.
She saw a sign
in a window.
The sign said
CHICKENS SERVED.

She went in
and sat down
at a table.

"I'm hungry,"
she said to the waiter.
"We serve chickens
to PEOPLE,"
the waiter told her.

"Then I guess
I had better leave,"
said Henrietta.

Some children were playing
in the street.
"Come play with us,"
they called to Henrietta.
"What can we play?"

"Let's have an egg hunt,"
said Henrietta.

"Where are the eggs?"
asked the children.
"I have them.
Close your eyes,"
Henrietta said.

Henrietta laid big eggs
and little eggs.
She laid red eggs
and pink, blue, and purple eggs.

40

She laid chocolate eggs.
She laid eggs with spots
and polka dots.

"I'm ready," she called.
"Find the eggs."

Just then
Mr. Gray drove up.
"WHAT are you doing, Henrietta?
Did you lay all those eggs?"
Mr. Gray asked.

"Yes," said Henrietta.
"Will you take me home?"
she asked.
"I'm tired.
It has been a long day."

"I sure will,"
said Mr. Gray.
"We can use more eggs
on the farm.
And little chicks too."

Henrietta was very glad
to be going home.

Henrietta, the Early Bird

Henrietta, the Early Bird

The sun was not up yet.
Everyone on the farm
was still asleep.

Henrietta opened her eyes.
She looked around.
She looked at the old clock.
Mr. Gray had left it there
the day before.

"Oh, my," said Henrietta.
"It's time to get up!
Something must have happened
to the rooster.
I'll wake the hens myself."

"Cock-a-doodle-doo!"
said Henrietta,
as loud as she could.

"You're not the rooster,
Henrietta,"
said the other hens.
They went back to sleep.

"Then I'll wake up the cows,"
said Henrietta.
She went to the barn.

"Cock-a-doodle-doo!"
said Henrietta,
as loud as she could.

"You're not the rooster,"
said the cows.
"But it's five o'clock,"
said Henrietta.
"It's time to get up."

"We'll wait for the rooster
to wake us up,"
said the cows.
They went back to sleep.

"I know the pigs
will listen to me,"
said Henrietta.
She went to the pigpen.

"Cock-a-doodle-doo!"
said Henrietta,
as loud as she could.
"It's time to get up."

"We heard you,"
said the pigs.
"Go back to bed.
We'll wait for the rooster
to wake us up."

The pigs went back to sleep.

"I'll go wake up Mr. Gray.
He'll know what to do,"
thought Henrietta.
She went to the farmhouse.

She jumped up on the window.

Mr. Gray was asleep.

"Cock-a-doodle-doo!"

said Henrietta,

as loud as she could.

Mr. Gray sat up in bed.

"What's that noise?" he asked.

Then he saw Henrietta

sitting on the windowsill.

"Cock-a-doodle-doo!"

she said again.

"Stop that noise, Henrietta,"
said Mr. Gray.
"Go back to bed."
He went back to sleep.

"What should I do now?"
Henrietta wondered.
"No one wants to get up."

She said, "Cock-a-doodle-doo!"
to the cat.
"Stop acting like a rooster,
Henrietta," said the cat.
"I don't want
to get up yet."

She said, "Cock-a-doodle-doo!"
to the dog.
"Please, Henrietta,"
said the dog,
"I want to sleep
a little longer."

Then Henrietta saw someone
moving in the field.
"Someone is awake at last,"
thought Henrietta.
She hurried to the field
to see who it was.

It was only the scarecrow
waving in the breeze.

"I'll try to wake everybody
one more time,"
thought Henrietta.
"Cock-a-doodle-doo!"
she shouted,
as loud as she could.

"Stop that, Henrietta,"
Mr. Gray called
from his window.
"We know it's you,
Henrietta,"
said the cows, pigs,
cat, dog, and other hens.
They all went back to sleep.

"Something is wrong.
Mr. Gray doesn't want
to get up.
The animals don't want
to get up.
I will go and get some help,"
thought Henrietta.
She hurried off to town.

But in town,
the streets were empty.
The houses were dark.

"Cock-a-doodle-doo!"
shouted Henrietta,
as loud as she could.

The lights came on.
People looked out
of their windows.
All they could see
was Henrietta.

"What are you doing
in town?"
asked the grown-ups.
"It's too early
to go to work."
They went back to bed.

"It's too early for us
to go to school
or start playing,"
said the children.
They went back to bed, too.

"If you make
any more noise,
I'll put you in jail,"
said a policeman.

Henrietta hurried
back to the farm.
"No one will help me,"
she thought.
"I'll just have to wake up
everyone on the farm myself."

As she was going
down the road,
she heard a loud
"Cock-a-doodle-doo!
Cock-a-doodle-doo!"

"The rooster is up,"
Henrietta thought happily.

"Good morning, Henrietta,"
said the rooster.
"I see you're up early today."
"I've been up
for a long time,"
said Henrietta.
"And I'm very tired."

Mr. Gray came out
of the farmhouse.
He was wide-awake now.

He fed the cat and dog.
He milked the cows
and let them
out of the barn.

He fed the pigs.

He went to the henhouse
to feed the chickens.
"You woke me up this morning,
Henrietta."

"Why did you make
so much noise?"
asked Mr. Gray.
"It was five o'clock,"
said Henrietta.
"It was time to get up."

"This old clock doesn't work,"
said Mr. Gray.
"You got up
in the middle of the night."
"No wonder I'm so sleepy,"
said Henrietta.

While the other hens ate,
Henrietta closed her eyes
and went to sleep.

"Cock-a-doodle-doo!"
shouted Mr. Gray.
All the animals made noise, too.
Henrietta flew up
in the air.
"I'll never get up
so early again," she said.

Henrietta
Goes to the Fair

Henrietta Goes to the Fair

"Today is the state fair,"
said Mr. Gray.
"Which of my animals
should I enter?
I'd like to win
a blue ribbon."

Henrietta heard him.
"Maybe he'll choose me,"
she thought.
"Everyone says
I'm a beautiful chicken."

First Mr. Gray looked at the cows.

Then he looked at his pigs.

Henrietta waited and waited.
"How about looking at us chickens?"
she asked.
But Mr. Gray didn't hear her.
He was still looking at the pigs.

"Winthrop, I think
you can win first prize today,"
said Mr. Gray.
"You are the biggest pig
I have ever seen.

I'll get my truck
and take you to the fair."
Mr. Gray went to get his truck.

"Good for you, Winthrop,"
said the cows.
"You'll win for our farm today."

"Yes, Winthrop,
we hope you'll win first prize,"
said the chickens.
"You are sure to win
a blue ribbon, Winthrop,"
said the other pigs.

"Good luck, Winthrop!"
said Henrietta.
"I hope you win, too."

Mr. Gray came back with his truck.

He helped Winthrop to get in.

"You sure are a big pig,"

Mr. Gray told Winthrop.

"There can't be

a bigger pig anywhere."

Mr. Gray drove off
down the road with Winthrop.
Henrietta walked away.
She was sorry
that she was not going
to the fair.

"I think I'll go and see
who Mr. Miller is taking
to the fair,"
said Henrietta.
She walked down the road
to Mr. Miller's farm.

At the gate
she saw a big sign.
It said: "KEEP OUT!"

Henrietta was very quiet
as she walked
toward the fence.

She peeked through a hole.
There stood
a very, very big pig.
It was the biggest pig
Henrietta had ever seen!

Mr. Miller came out
of his house.
He did not see Henrietta.

"Come on, Melvin,
it's time to go
to the fair,"
he said.
"You are sure to win
first prize."

He helped Melvin
to get into the truck.

"Oh, my," thought Henrietta,
"Winthrop will never win.
I must tell Mr. Gray."

Henrietta jumped
into the back of the truck.

"Move over, Melvin,"
she said.
"I'm going to the fair, too."

When they got to the fair,
she hopped off the truck.

She ran. She flew.

"Where are they showing the pigs?"
Henrietta asked.

People didn't answer.
They were too busy
eating candy and ice cream.

Then Henrietta
saw some children on a ride.
"Have you seen the pigs?"
she asked.
The children
didn't hear her.

They were going
around and around
on the merry-go-round.
Henrietta went
around and around too.

She was dizzy
when she got off.

"Excuse me,
have you seen the pigs?"
Henrietta asked.
"No, I'm judging apple pies,"
said the woman.

"Do you know
where the pigs are?"
Henrietta asked.
"No, I'm picking
the best pickles,"
said another woman.

At last Henrietta saw
a big sign.
It said: "PIGS."

"There's Winthrop!"
said Henrietta.

Just then the judges said,
"The blue ribbon
for the biggest pig
in the state goes to—
Mr. Miller's pig, Melvin!"

Mr. Gray looked very sad.

So did Winthrop.

"That's all right, Winthrop,"
said Mr. Gray.

"You weren't the biggest pig."

Henrietta was sad too.
She went over and sat
with the other chickens.

The judges came along
to pick the best chicken.
"How can we pick the best?"
they said.

Then they saw Henrietta.
"You are a beautiful chicken,"
said the judges.

"Me?" said Henrietta.

The judges put the blue ribbon
around Henrietta's neck.

Henrietta ran
to Mr. Gray and Winthrop.
"Look! Look!" said Henrietta.
"I'm the best chicken.
I've won first prize!"

Mr. Gray was very happy.
But Winthrop
still looked sad.

"Thanks to Henrietta
I did win a blue ribbon!"
said Mr. Gray.
He patted Henrietta
on the head.

"And I'm sure
that Winthrop will win
next year!"
"I'm sure
he will win, too,"
said Henrietta.

On the way
back to the farm
Henrietta said,
"It was a great day
at the fair!"